W9-DFF-164

LITTLE SIMON

An imprint of Simon & Schuster Children's Publishing Division • 1230 Avenue of the Americas, New York, New York 10020 • First Little Simon hardcover edition August 2016 • Copyright © 2016 by Simon & Schuster, Inc. All rights reserved, including the right of reproduction in whole or in part in any form. LITTLE SIMON is a registered trademark of Simon & Schuster, Inc., and associated colophon is a trademark of Simon & Schuster, Inc. For information about special discounts for bulk purchases, please contact Simon & Schuster Special Sales at 1-866-506-1949 or business@simonandschuster.com. The Simon & Schuster Speakers Bureau can bring authors to your live event. For more information or to book an event contact the Simon & Schuster Speakers Bureau at 1-866-248-3049 or visit our website at www.simonspeakers.com. Designed by Laura Roode. The text of this book was set in Usherwood. Manufactured in the United States of America 0716 FFG

10 9 8 7 6 5 4 3 2 1

Cataloging-in-Publication Data for this title is available from the Library of Congress.

ISBN 978-1-4814-6699-8 (hc)
ISBN 978-1-4814-6698-1 (pbk)
ISBN 978-1-4814-6700-1 (eBook)

the adventures of
SOPHIE MOUSE
8

A surprise visitor

By Poppy Green • Illustrated by Jennifer A. Bell

LITTLE SIMON
New York London Toronto Sydney New Delhi

Contents

chapter 1

Party Time!

All week long, Sophie had been look-ing forward to Saturday.

Now—*finally*—the day was here. The Mouse family was having a dinner party. Their guests would be arriving any minute!

Sophie studied the dining table. She wanted to make sure everything was perfect.

"Oh! The place cards!" Sophie said suddenly. "How could I forget?"

She scurried up to her bedroom. On her drawing table were ten cards, set out to dry. Sophie had painted them by hand.

Back downstairs, Sophie walked around the table. She smiled as she put down the first card. It read HARRIET in neat brush strokes. The *I* was dotted with a flower. Sophie was one of few who knew her best friend Hattie Frog's real name.

At another spot, Sophie put down a place card for

her other best friend, Owen Snake. She had made a smiley face inside the *o*.

"I'll put *my* place card right between theirs," Sophie decided. She'd get to sit next to both of them!

She knew her little brother, Winston, would want to sit near them. So Sophie put his card at the spot right across from her own. She put the place card for Hattie's big sister, Lydie, across from Hattie.

Finally, she placed the cards for the grown-ups: George and Lily Mouse, Mr. and Mrs. Frog, and Mrs. Snake.

"There!" Sophie said. "Now everything is ready."

"Good!" said Winston. He was peering out the front window. "Because here they come!"

Sophie and Winston raced to the door. *Good hosts always give their guests a warm welcome!* Sophie thought.

She flung the door open. "Hello everyone!" she called.

"Sophie!" Hattie and Owen cried and ran toward her. Their families were right behind them.

Sophie welcomed all the guests.
She and Winston took coats while
George and Lily Mouse came out
from the kitchen to say hello.

Sophie and Winston had already

decided that the kids would play a game of hide-and-seek. It was one of their favorites! Sophie drew the short stick and had to be the seeker. But she didn't complain. She knew a good host probably shouldn't.

When it was
time for dinner,
Sophie helped
everyone find
their place.
She poured
water from
the walnut jug
into the acorn cups. Then she helped

her parents serve the food.

Before Sophie knew it, it was time for dessert. She jumped up from the table as her parents cleared the

dishes. Because she—Sophie Mouse—
had made the dessert *all by herself.*
She could not wait for everyone to
see it!

Sophie hurried down into the root
cellar. She opened
the icebox. Very
carefully, she
took out the
trifle. It was
made of eight
layers of sponge
cake, berries, and
whipped cream.
They made a

pretty pattern through the sides of
the glass bowl.

Sophie climbed up the cellar
stairs. She grinned,
imagining what
everyone would
say. As she
reached the
top step, she
called out,
"Time for
dessert!"

Only it *wasn't* the top step. There was one more step. And Sophie tripped on it. The serving bowl went flying. Sophie lunged for it. She got a grip on the base. But then the

whole bowl turned upside down. The contents of the bowl tipped over and—

SPLAT!

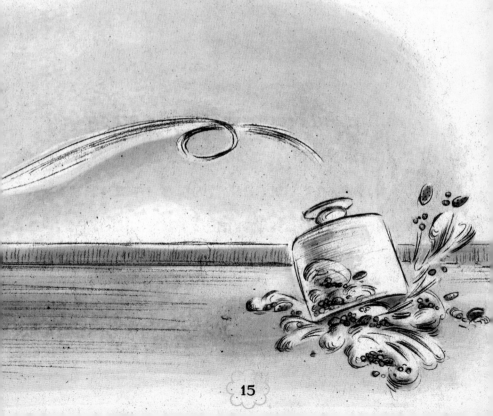

Whipped cream, berries, and cake
fell in a heap at Sophie's feet.

All heads turned. For a moment,
no one spoke. Surprised faces looked
from Sophie to the dessert puddle—
and back again.

Sophie felt like crying. Her whole

dessert—it was ruined! But Sophie took a deep breath and tried to stay calm. She figured that's what a good host would do.

"Well, I guess we're having tea for dessert," she said, forcing a smile.

chapter 2

Daydream
Surprise

After all the guests had left, Sophie got her sketchbook and sat on the couch, drawing. Winston picked out a book and plopped down next to her. Lily Mouse was putting away leftovers from dinner. George Mouse was drying the dishes.

"What a nice party we had," Mrs. Mouse said.

Sophie groaned. "Except for when I dropped the dessert!" she said.

Mr. Mouse came over and squeezed Sophie's shoulder. "I know it was disappointing after all your hard work, but you handled it very well, Sophie."

Mrs. Mouse hung up her apron. "We can have guests again soon," she said gently. "And you can make the trifle again! You're a pro now."

Sophie had had the same idea. She was already dreaming about what the new and *improved* trifle would be like.

The next day Mr. Mouse was getting ready for a work meeting. He'd finished the blueprints for a new birdhouse and was going to show the family. It was going to have a convertible roof that could be opened on warm, sunny days.

Mrs. Mouse announced she was going out too. "I need to stop by the berry patch. There are lots of berries in my recipes for this week," she explained. Mrs. Mouse owned the bakery in Pine Needle Grove, and she was always coming up with deli-cious—and imagina-tive—new treats.

Winston wanted to go too. "I'll come

and help!" he exclaimed. Sophie bet he was *really* thinking about the berries he could eat as he picked.

Sophie decided to stay home. She had her sketchpad at the dining table and wanted to finish her drawing.

So the rest of the family went off. Sophie was on her own for the afternoon. She didn't mind one bit.

With the house quiet, Sophie just sat for a while. Her sketchbook lay open in her lap. But she gazed out the window and let her mind wander into a daydream.

The sky is so blue today, she

thought. *I wonder what that color looks like to birds up in the sky. If blue is all around you, does it look more blue because there's so much of it? Or less blue because there are no other colors to compare it to?*

From there, Sophie daydreamed about being able to fly. She pictured herself perched on a tree branch. She flapped her wings. Her feet lifted off the branch. She was flying—but just barely. And it was so much work!

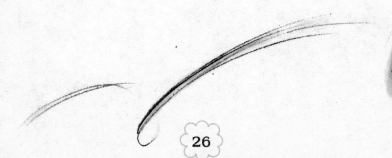

Her wings were getting tired. But now there was nothing nearby to land on! She was sinking lower and lower in the air. She started to tumble down, head over feet, until—

WHOMP!

Sophie snapped out of her day-dream. What was that sound? Was it in her daydream? Or had it actually

happened? Sophie was almost certain she had really heard it.

But where had the noise come from?

— chapter 3 —

Follow That Sound!

Sophie's whiskers twitched. The rest of her was absolutely still. She waited for the sound to repeat.

She could hear trees rustling in the breeze outside.

She could hear the ticking of the clock on a shelf.

Then Sophie's ears perked up at a different sound.

Chirrrrrrp.

Of course, chirps were not an unusual sound around here. The Mouse family had lots of bird neighbors. But this chirp was particularly long and low-pitched for a chirp. To Sophie, it sounded kind of sad.

It also sounded particularly close. Almost as if it was coming from *inside* the house. Sophie's heart beat a little faster. Was there someone else in the house?

Chirrrrrrp.

There it was again! Sophie turned toward the staircase. That time it

sounded like it was coming from the second floor.

Slowly, warily, Sophie climbed the stairs. At the top, she peered around the corner. She could see all the way down the hall. There was no one there.

Chirrrrrrp.

This one was even louder. *I'm getting closer!* Sophie figured.

She tiptoed to the doorway of her

parents' bedroom. She peeked inside.
No sign of anyone.

Next she came to Winston's room.
No one.

Chirp. Chirrrrrrp.

Sophie glanced toward the end of the hall. *That one definitely sounded like it came from my room!* she thought.

Sophie scurried to her open door. She didn't see anyone inside. She entered her room and flung open her closet. She looked under her bed. She

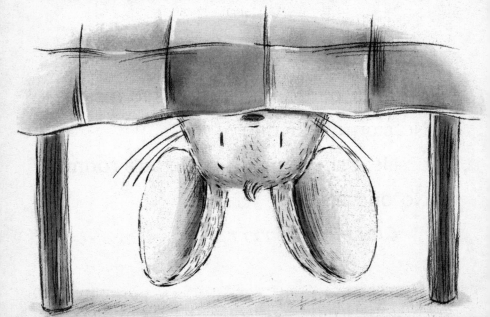

looked behind her
drawing table. But
her bedroom
seemed just
the same as
always.

Sophie was
puzzled. She
sat down on
her bed to think.

Chirrrrrrp.

Sophie jumped up. She followed
the sound to the open window.

Sophie leaned on the windowsill
and poked her head out. She looked

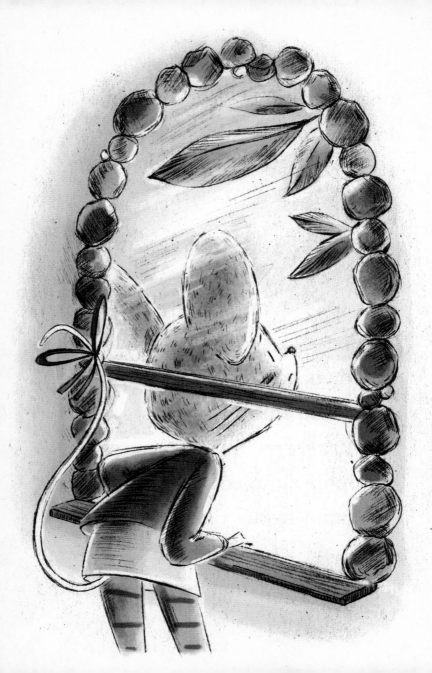

up into the branches of the trees.

Suddenly, a voice came from some-where quite close to her!

Chirp. "H-hello?"

Sophie jumped in surprise. She hit the back of her head on the raised window. "Ow!" she cried.

"Oh! Are you okay?" the little voice asked. "So sorry to startle you!"

Rubbing her head, Sophie leaned back out to see who was there.

chapter 4

Sophie to the Rescue

A small bird was sitting on the section of the roof over the Mouse family's living room. Since there was no second floor above it, the bird was at the same level as Sophie's window.

"Are—are you okay?" Sophie asked the bird.

The bird looked down at his left wing. "Well. N-not exactly," he said

with another gloomy chirp. "My wing really hurts. I don't think I can fly right now. So . . ." He peered nervously down over the roof's edge. "I think I'm stuck up here."

Sophie looked around. She couldn't just *leave* the little bird. But how could she help him get down safely?

Suddenly Sophie remembered something.

"Hold on!" she called to the bird. "I'll be right there."

Sophie hurried downstairs and

out the front door. She ran around the side of the house. At a certain point, the house nestled up against the trunk of the oak tree. She stopped at the intersection and looked up at the roof. There was the bird! She waved.

Then Sophie started climbing the tree trunk. Her feet easily found a series of footholds carved into the bark.

Together, the footholds formed a
kind of ladder. It led right up to the
roof of the house.

Before she knew it, Sophie had
climbed to the roof level. From there,
she could reach out and touch the bird.

"How did you do that?" the bird asked her.

Sophie smiled. "My dad made this ladder years ago," she explained. "He was fixing the roof. It made the job easier. I'm glad I remembered it was here!"

Sophie had lots of questions for the bird. But she could see that now was not the time. So she just asked his name.

"It's Finch," he said with a shy smile.

"Hi, Finch. I'm Sophie," she said cheerfully. "Now let's get you down from here!"

Sophie helped Finch get his legs on the top two footholds of the ladder. Then Sophie went first and very slowly helped guide Finch down. She supported his weight, since he could use only one wing.

When they got to the ground, they
both sighed with relief.

"Thank you so much!" said Finch.

"Of course," Sophie replied. "So . . .
what happened? How did you get
stuck up on our roof?"

chapter 5

Finch's Story

Finch looked down at the ground. He seemed embarrassed. "Well, I was playing hide-and-seek with my friends—"

"That's funny!" Sophie said. "I just played hide-and-seek with my friends last night! We love that game." Then she realized she had interrupted. "Sorry. Go on."

Finch smiled.
"Well, I flew off
to find a hiding
spot. Maybe
I flew too far.
But anyway, I
hid and I waited.
No one came to
find me. So I flew
back toward home base. But I got
totally lost. I was looking for familiar trees and then all of a sudden I
got knocked out of the air. I think it
was a branch that came loose. And
I fell right onto your roof."

"Oh dear," said Sophie. "That branch! What bad luck!"

Finch nodded. "Thanks again for helping me down. I don't know what I would have done."

Sophie invited Finch inside. "Are

you hungry?" she asked him. "My mom made some muffins this morning. She runs the bakery in Pine Needle Grove."

Finch followed behind her. "I've never been to Pine Needle Grove. I live on Sugar Maple Lane. Have you heard of it?"

Sophie shook her head no. "And I'm not sure I've ever met a finch before!" she said excitedly.

Finch laughed. "Actually, I'm not

a finch. I'm a blue-winged warbler."
He shrugged. "My parents named
me Finch after a friend of theirs."

"Oh, how nice!" Sophie exclaimed.
"I don't know where my name came
from. But my little brother, Winston,
couldn't pronounce it when he was
a baby. He
used to say
'Thophie,'"
she said,
laughing
as she
remembered.

Finch laughed too.

Sophie found a tin of muffins and offered one to Finch. He reached for it with his left wing. "Ouch!" he cried.

"Oh no," Sophie said. "Does it hurt a lot?"

Finch rubbed his hurt wing with his other wing. "Not when I don't try to move it," he said.

"Hmm," said Sophie. "Then maybe we should keep you from moving it. You need a sling!"

Sophie started looking around the room for something to use.

"What's a sling?" Finch asked as she scurried about.

Sophie explained. "It'll take some weight off your wing. And it will remind you not to use it. My brother had one after he twisted his wrist."

Sophie looked and looked. She searched upstairs, too. But she couldn't find anything right for a sling.

Then a leaf blew in through an open window. "Aha!" she said. "I should look *outside*! I'll be right back!"

Sophie ran out the front door. She found a large, soft wild ginger leaf that was just the right size. She also

picked two long blades of grass.

Back inside, Sophie gently wrapped
the leaf around Finch's wing. She used
the grass to hold the sling in place,
tying the blades behind his neck.

"There!" said Sophie. "That should

keep your wing protected. At least
while we figure out what to do."

Finch nodded.

Sophie smiled.

Finch shrugged, then said, "So,
what *should* we do?"

chapter 6

A Picture of Home

Sophie wondered if they should go find her mom or dad. But she wasn't *exactly* sure where her dad's meeting was. As for finding her mom, the berry patch was a long walk. And there were a few ways to get there. What if they set out one way while Mrs. Mouse and Winston were coming home another way?

Meanwhile, Finch was looking around. "Your house is really nice," he said. "It's so different than mine."

"Thanks!" Sophie replied. "My dad designed it. He's an architect."

Sophie gave Finch a tour. She showed him the root cellar, and the little porch, and the upstairs, including her room. Finch asked about her art table.

"I really love to draw and paint," Sophie explained. "So I also call this my *studio*!"

Finch pointed to some paintings on a shelf. "Did you paint all these?" he asked.

Sophie nodded. "Yep! Most of them are places I've been."

Finch looked very impressed. "You're really good!"

"Thanks!" Sophie said proudly.

Finch looked more closely at each painting—one by one. There

was the painting of the buttercup patch, where Owen had rescued her from a hole. One of Weedsnag Way, where she and Hattie had found the emerald berries. There was Forget-Me-Not Lake and Hickory Hill, and more. Looking at them helped Sophie remember all of her adventures so clearly.

Finch turned to Sophie. "Would you do a painting . . . for *me*?" he asked.

Sophie beamed. "I'd love to!" she replied. "I could do it right now!"

So Sophie got out a blank piece of paper. She clipped it to her easel. She got her brushes and paints ready.

Then she looked at Finch. "Tell me about Sugar Maple Lane," she said.

Finch thought about it for a minute. Then he described the view from his family's front porch. From there, he could see all the way down Sugar Maple Lane.

"It's a row of six sugar maple trees," Finch said. "In each one, there is a layer of branches that line up perfectly with the other trees' branches. Dozens of bird families have built their houses there. So it's like any neighborhood— it's just way up above the ground."

Finch described many more details: the colors, the shapes, the textures of his world. He watched Sophie add them to the scene.

"Wow," said Sophie when they finished. "Sugar Maple Lane is beautiful. I need to come and visit sometime!"

Finch flapped his good wing. "You should!" he replied. "I would love to host you at *my* house."

Hearing the word "host," Sophie suddenly realized something.

"Of course!" she exclaimed. "I am your host! That means *you* are my *guest*!"

Finch looked confused.

Sophie headed for the kitchen.

"Come on, Finch! I know exactly what we should do next!"

chapter 7

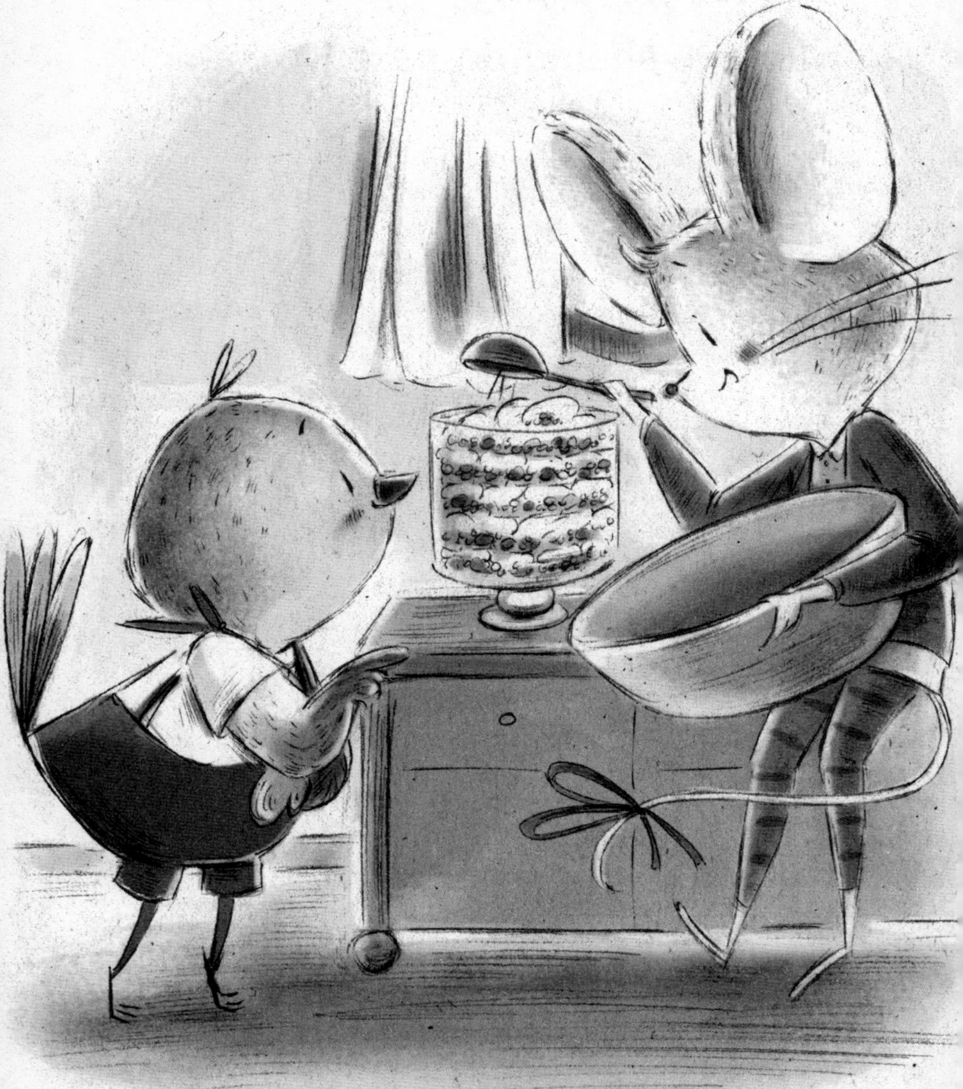

More Visitors?

Finch rubbed his belly. "That looks so delicious," he said to Sophie.

She was scraping the last scoop of whipped cream out of the mixing bowl. She plopped it on top of the dessert.

"It's called a trifle," Sophie said. "And I think this one turned out even better than yesterday's."

Sophie had told Finch the whole story. She told him about the dinner party the night before. She told him about the beautiful dessert she'd made.

She told him how she had dropped it all over the floor.

Then, together, Sophie and Finch had remade the trifle.

Sophie scooped the delicious-looking dessert into two bowls, one for each of them. Then they dug in.

And it *tasted* just as delicious as it looked!

As Sophie took her last bite, there was a knock at the door. She jumped up from her chair. "Maybe it's Mom or Dad!" she cried. "But wait. Why would they knock?"

Sophie hurried to the door and peeked out. On the doorstep were three young birds. Sophie didn't recognize them.

"Yes?" she asked uncertainly.

The orange bird in the middle cleared her throat. "Um. Hello. My name is Ginger. I'm looking for my friend. He's a blue-winged warbler and his name is Finch. I don't suppose—"

Sophie gasped and flung the door wide open. Finch came running up behind Sophie.

"Ginger!" he cried. "Max! Lewis!"

All three of the birds were

overjoyed to see Finch. Then they
noticed the sling on his wing.

Ginger gasped. "What happened?
Are you okay?"

Finch looked embarrassed again.
"I had a . . . hard landing," he said.

Then he pointed to Sophie. "But luckily, I landed on *Sophie's* house. She really helped me out."

Finch introduced Sophie to each of his friends. "Nice to meet you!" Sophie said.

Now I have four *guests!* Sophie thought. This was turning into a

party. She was so glad she had made the trifle!

"Is anybody hungry?" Sophie asked.

chapter 8

First, Dessert!

While Sophie served the trifle, the birds took turns telling their stories. Finch told his friends how he'd gotten lost, been hit by the branch, and wound up hurt on Sophie's roof.

"How did you find me?" Finch asked his friends.

Ginger explained they'd been looking all over for him. "At first we just

thought you had a really great hiding place," she said.

Max added, "Then it seemed like something must have happened."

"So we flew around in circles, searching for you," said Lewis. "Finally, Ginger spotted a few feathers on the roof of this house."

Ginger held the feathers up. "Look familiar?" she asked Finch with a grin. "We weren't sure they were yours. But we thought we should check it out."

Soon all the dessert bowls were empty. Lewis patted his belly. "Wow! That was so yummy!" he exclaimed. Ginger and Max agreed. Finch put his good wing on Sophie's shoulder. "It's called trifle," he said, proud to share his new knowledge. "We made it this afternoon."

Ginger looked outside. "Uh-oh. It's getting late," she said. "I think we'd better head home."

"Yeah," said Max. "My mom told me to be back for dinner."

"Mine too," Finch said. "But . . ." He looked down at his sling. "I don't think I can fly. My wing still hurts a lot. How am I going to get home?"

Sophie and the others were

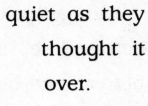

quiet as they thought it over.

"I wish I knew the way," Sophie said. "I could tell you how to walk home."

Ginger frowned. "Though that would take a lot longer than flying," she pointed out. "We might not make it there before dark."

Lewis crouched down with his back to Finch. "Hop on my back," Lewis told

him. "Maybe I could carry you."

Finch climbed on. Lewis's legs trembled a bit. He could hold Finch. But when he flapped his wings, Lewis couldn't get off the ground.

"Nope, I can't do it," said Lewis. "At least, not by myself."

But Lewis's idea gave *Sophie* an idea. "Maybe you could *all* carry him—together?" Her eyes fell on Finch's sling. "That's it!"

Sophie rushed upstairs and opened the hall closet. She pulled out a dandelion-fluff blanket and carried it downstairs. "Come on!" she called

to the others as she led them outside.

Sophie spread the blanket out on the ground. "Finch sits in the center," she explained. "Then each of you grab a corner or side of the blanket in your beak. When you take flight, you'll lift Finch up!"

Lewis gasped. "It's like a big sling!" he cried.

"Exactly!" said Sophie.

Ginger and Max nodded and smiled.

Finch was the only one who didn't seem excited. In fact, he looked pretty nervous.

He shook his head and backed away from the blanket. "What if I fall out? What if you drop me? I don't think I can get in there."

What were they going to do now?

when mice fly . . .

"You're right," Ginger said matter-of-factly. "You're not getting in there. Not until we test it. We need to make sure it's safe."

Sophie liked Ginger. She reminded Sophie of Hattie—practical and very cautious.

"Good idea!" said Sophie. She picked up a large rock and put it at the center of the blanket.

Ginger, Max, and Lewis grabbed different corners of the blanket in their beaks.

"Ready?" Sophie called out. "One! Two! Three!"

The birds flapped their wings. They rose into the air. The sling cradled the rock inside. It was working!

Ginger, Max, and Lewis flew slowly in a wide circle, practicing. They had to fly close together to keep

the rock cradled. But they had no
trouble at all. The rock seemed safe
and secure.

Then they came in for a landing, carefully setting the rock down
before they landed themselves.

"That was great!" Sophie exclaimed.
She turned to Finch. "What do you
think?"

Finch still looked nervous. "I don't know . . ."

"Really?" said Sophie. She knew Finch was probably still rattled from his accident. But Sophie couldn't hide her enthusiasm. "It looks so fun! I'd get in there in a second."

Finch's eyes went wide with surprise. "You would?"

"Sure!" Sophie replied. "In fact, why *don't* I try it? I've always wanted to know what it would feel like to fly!"

The birds giggled at her eagerness.

"Let's do it!" cried Ginger.

Ginger, Max, and Lewis took their places again. They grabbed the corners of the blanket. Sophie felt the fabric hugging her on all sides, then lifting her off the ground.

"Whoo-hoo!" Sophie cried out. "Be back in a minute, Finch!"

At first the birds flew fairly low to the ground. The wind ruffled Sophie's fur. The blanket swung left and right

as the birds swooped this way and
that. Sophie peeked over the top of
the blanket.

"I'm flying!" she yelled. "Yippeeee!"

The birds carried her higher into

the air. Sophie looked down. She could
see the roof of her house. She could
see Hattie's house and the stream.
They went even higher. Sophie could
see some of the buildings in town and

even parts of Forget-Me-Not-Lake.

"Wow," Sophie whispered in awe. She had been high up on a Ferris wheel before. But this felt different. She knew it was the closest she'd ever get to being able to fly herself. She studied the blue sky. It didn't look any more or less blue than from the ground, but somehow it seemed even more beautiful. She loved being able to see the treetops, and her fellow ground-dwellers down below. She even thought she could see Hattie playing near her house. She couldn't *wait* to tell Hattie all about her day.

Too soon, the birds came in for a landing next to Finch. They lowered Sophie gently onto the ground. Then they let go of the corners. The blanket unfurled, and Sophie jumped out.

"Amazing!" she cried. "You guys are so lucky that this is how you get around!"

The birds laughed.

"Okay," said Finch. "I think I'm ready."

chapter 10

Finch's Farewell

Finch took a deep breath. He stepped onto the blanket.

And just like that, Sophie realized it was time to say good-bye.

"Oh, wait!" she cried suddenly. "Don't go yet!"

She ran into her house and up to her room. The painting of Sugar Maple Lane was still sitting on her

easel. She gently touched it to make
sure it was dry. Then she rolled it up
and tied it with a blade of grass.

Sophie carried it outside. "You
can't forget this!" Sophie said, hand-
ing it to him. "It's all dry. Just make

sure to unroll it when you get home
so it lays flat!"

Finch smiled. "Thank you, Sophie!"
he said. "For everything." He gave
her a one-winged hug.

"I hope your wing feels better soon," Sophie replied.

Finch nodded. "I'm sure it will. And then I can come back and visit again."

Ginger, Max, and Lewis agreed. "We'll come along and show Finch how to get here," Ginger said.

Sophie clapped excitedly. "I can't wait!" she replied.

Ginger, Max, and Lewis grabbed the corners of the blanket. Sophie waved as they lifted Finch up into the air. She kept on waving as the birds flew higher and higher, and disappeared into the trees.

Then, as Sophie Mouse turned to
go inside, she heard a familiar sound.
It was Winston's voice echoing down
the forest path. He and Mom were
home!

Sophie ran down the path to meet them. She was eager to tell them all about her guests—and her stay-at-home adventure.

The End

You'll also enjoy

the adventures of 9

SOPHIE MOUSE

The Great Big Paw Print

by Poppy Green • illustrated by Jennifer A. Bell

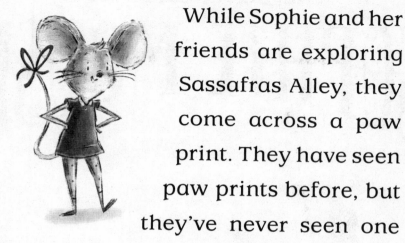

While Sophie and her friends are exploring Sassafras Alley, they come across a paw print. They have seen paw prints before, but they've never seen one this *big*! What sort of animal could possibly have made such a giant paw print? As the friends go on an adventure to find out, they are in for a great big surprise!

the adventures of
SOPHIE MOUSE

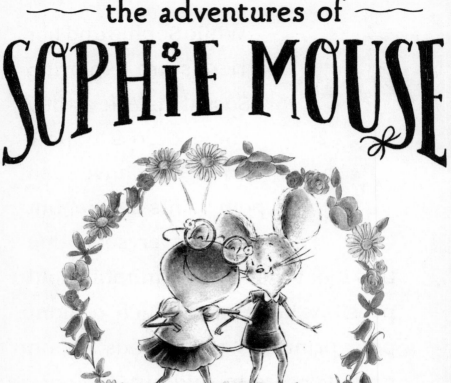

For excerpts, activities, and more about
these adorable tales & tails, visit
AdventuresofSophieMouse.com!